## Dedication

This book is for the Mom's.
More specifically, The Pandemic Mom's.
We are extraordinary people with
extraordinary families
and an extraordinary story to tell.


I also dedicate this book to my son, Bobby.
You are such a wild, beautiful bub.
You've given this cold world
more gifts than it deserves
by just being you.

To request permissions, contact the publisher at paperenergycollective@gmail.com

Paperback: ISBN 978-1-7379590-0-7

Library of Congress Control Number: 2021921008

First paperback edition: November 2021

Cover art done in collaboration with Elizabeth Peteya, sister & friend
Layout by Shane Saldivar, Creative Consultant
About the Author written by Sabrina Lee O. Sanchez, friend

Printed by IngramSpark in the USA

# Essential Love:

## A Mom's Story

By: Jennifer "Punch" Parchment

It's a BOY...
It's a GIRL...
It's a **PANDEMIC?!**

# The year was 2020.

The president was orange
people were blue
strangers marched together
in other words, a big hullabaloo.

Yet heroes fought the good fight
cloaked in masks and sci-fi fashion
goodness was everywhere in sight
and staying safe became our passion.

Every evening a series of BRAVOS!
echoed through the quiet streets
for all the heroes and essential workers
who never missed a single beat.

Loud pans and pots click-clanged
and proud, joyous signs were hanged.

But behind many a lawn poster
lived loving, worried parents
on an emotional roller-coaster.

These moms and dads
were another type of hero
crammed inside four walls
where privacy was zero.

Although some would decree
        the hardest role
belonged to the Moms 2 Be.

Those with new life in their bellies
hunkered down at home
trying to stay safe
but only for so long.

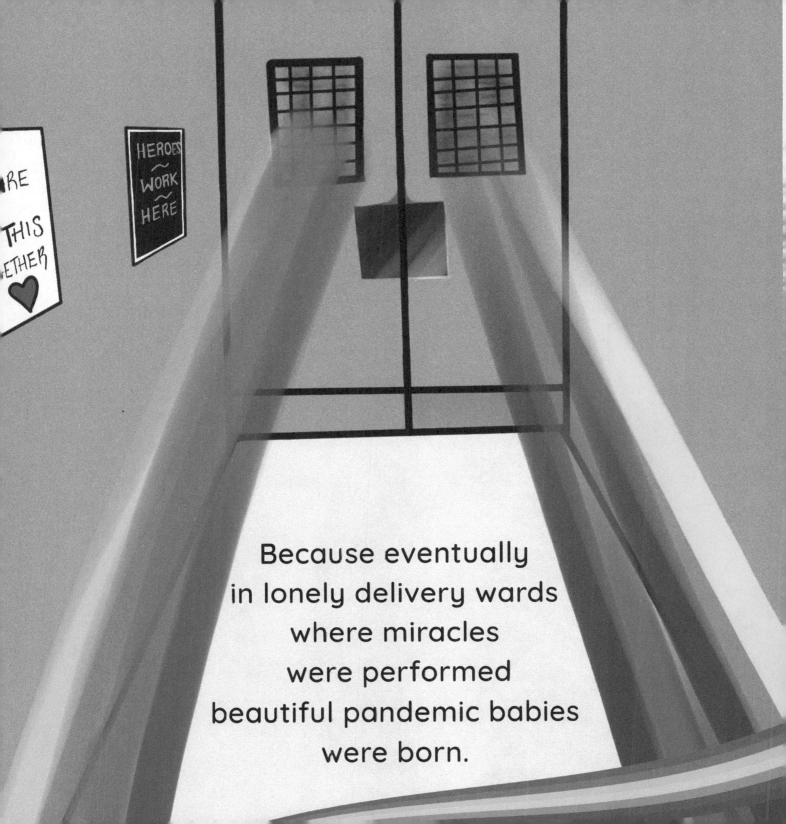

Because eventually
in lonely delivery wards
where miracles
were performed
beautiful pandemic babies
were born.

Magical babies destined for greatness
and maybe a special power or two
you see these newborns were able to talk
but only to the first person they knew.

To their mommas of course,
and their first words
were "I Love You."

These words and their surreal delivery
from babies who aren't supposed to speak
wasn't lost on these moms
who were trying not to freak.

Moms stuck at home
with crazy mom-buns
unshowered wondrous bodies
and stress by the ton.

These moms
needed these babies
as much as the babies
needed their mommas.

And the words these babies delivered
became their beautiful mama mantras.

# Momma, repeat after me:

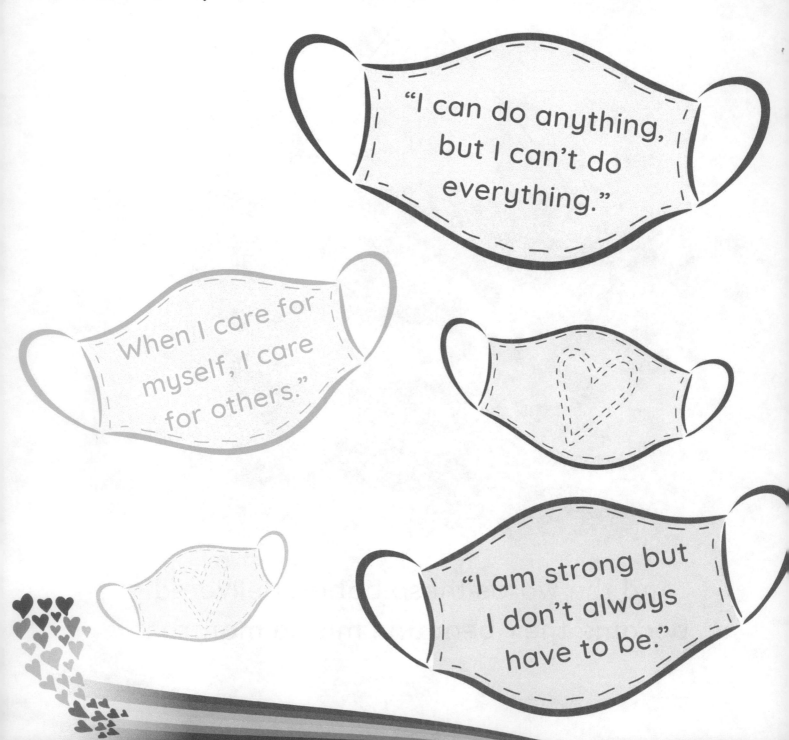

"I can do anything, but I can't do everything."

When I care for myself, I care for others."

"I am strong but I don't always have to be."

"I choose love and love chooses me."

"I have enough,
I do enough,
I am enough."

# Momma, repeat after me:

"This is hard, but I can do hard things."

"Life does not have to be perfect to be wonderful."

# Momma, repeat after me:

# "I LOVE YOU!"

...they would say to each other.

As more pandemic babies were born
the number of mantras grew
customized for each loving momma
courtesy of the baby she brewed.

Mommas began to take heed
to the mantras they repeated
these mom's had gotten what they needed
and slowly felt less and less defeated.

Momma's taking pride in what they've done and even more importantly...what they've OVERCOME.

An earth shattering event
that couldn't shatter their spirit
where moms stood strong
and the world needed to hear it!

And once things were lifted
their love and confidence endured

All thanks to their
special, magical babies
for that we are sure!

THE END

# Acknowledgements

**Rob** - You have always been my light. When everything felt groggy, dismal and dark, there you stood with the biggest and brightest torch to help see me through. You are the best thing that's ever happened to me.

**Elizabeth** - You've seen me at my worst and loved me anyway. I will always appreciate you for spending 99% of your summer quarantine days on the other side of the phone with me. You are someone who's seen vulnerability and fragility in me. You applaud it, you love it, you support it. And I see true humanity, love and support in you.

**Our Family** - Thank you for wearing masks around Bobby for one full year. You all never questioned our desire to keep Bobby safe. I was able to preserve the small sanity I had remaining in 2020 because you kept showing up for us time and time again. We love you forever!

**My Women Warriors** - To the ones who love me fiercely and without fail, YOU ALL MAKE ME GREAT! Despite your own struggles, you checked in. Day in and day out. I'm in awe of the women you all are. Despite your own "stuff," you saw me struggling and chose to LEAN IN. You are incredible.

**My Tribe** - A tribe is loosely defined as a group who has the same interests. I'd go so far to say that everyone in our tribe also has the same heart. We are better together. From those who dropped off masks and gloves in the early days, to the folks who continued to visit even when we made them social distance in our house. We're all better humans and friends accordingly.

**Shane** - A furlough brought us together... and now a book will forever bind us. Pun intended. Thanks for believing in me as I will always believe in you. This book would not exist in this beautiful way without all of your hard work.

# About the Author

Jenn (Punch) Parchment is a native New Yorker, with a distinct accent that tells you exactly where she's from. And, if you can't hear that accent, you're probably not from New York.

In Spring 2020, New York City became one of many global epicenters for COVID-19. Seven months pregnant (and counting) during a pandemic, Jenn put on a brave, masked face as she continued her daily treks into her Tribeca office.

However when the city started to shut down, Jenn began working from home while her husband Rob, kept up his daily shifts in NYC corrections.

Despite social distancing, constantly sanitizing and masking to the high heavens, Rob tested positive for COVID-19 just weeks before their son Bobby's arrival. Then while in labor, the frantic soon-to-be parents were wrecked when Jenn also tested positive for COVID-19.

With a devastating dual diagnosis, Jenn & Rob told their bad thoughts to take a backseat as they welcomed the most perfect human on Friday, May 8th 2020. The heir to the throne, Bobby Parchment a/k/a RP3.

Jenn's daily thoughts and musings about parenthood became Essential Love - A Mom's Story, a children's book written with new mothers as its primary audience.

Memorializing the events of 2020 in such an innocuous way via "Essential Love", serves to acknowledge our collective experience and reinforces the compassion we are capable of having for each other. In the end, we are mostly just flawed human beings trying our best to make it through [insert difficult time].

When she's not running around with Bobby, or constantly laughing with Rob, Jenn Punch can be found in the middle of the dance floor, the life of any party.

CPSIA information can be obtained
at www.ICGtesting.com
Printed in the USA
BVHW012300151121
621747BV00013B/453

9 781737 959007